On Wings of Grace

by
Bobbi Clavette

Illustrated by Jordan Harbin

AuthorHouse™
1663 Liberty Drive
Bloomington, IN 47403
www.authorhouse.com
Phone: 1 (800) 839-8640

Published by AuthorHouse 04/23/2019

ISBN: 978-1-7283-0819-7 (sc)
ISBN: 978-1-7283-0820-3 (hc)
ISBN: 978-1-7283-0818-0 (e)

Library of Congress Control Number: 2019904476

Print information available on the last page.

This book is printed on acid-free paper.

authorHOUSE®

Peeping through the opening was a hairy, spotted little caterpillar named Emmy Jo.

Exhausted and alone, she crawled beneath a leaf and began to cry.

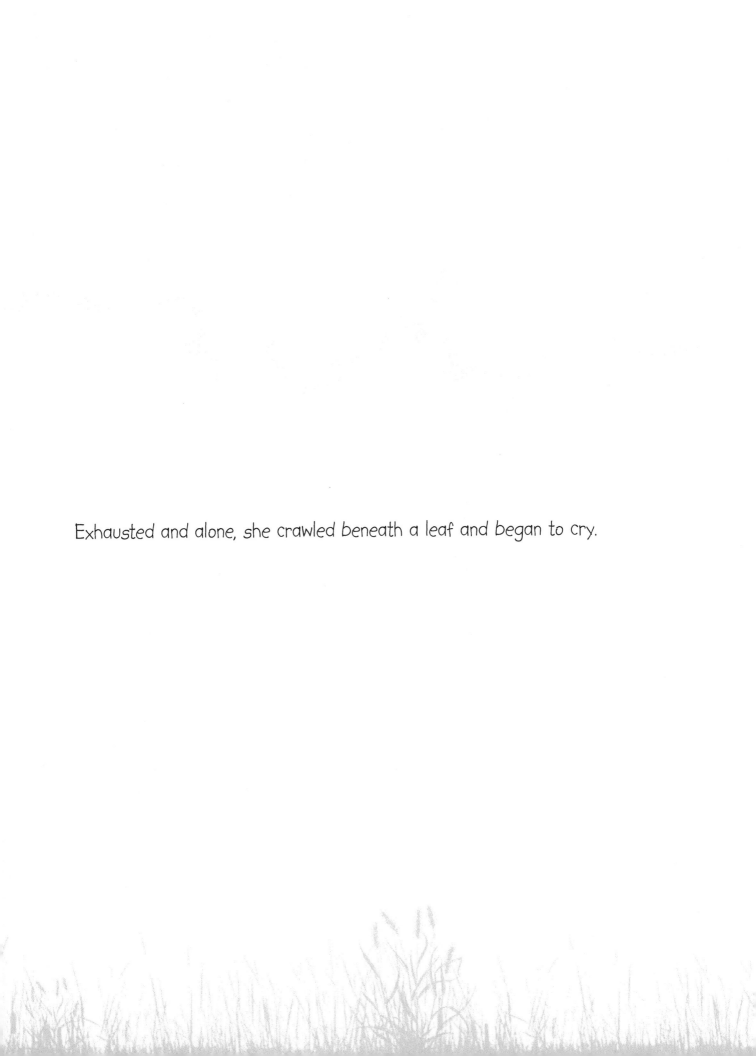

Emmy crawled up the grape vine she once called home.

Feeling life was too hard to continue, she considered her options. While thinking, she overheard chatter coming from a nearby vine. She could not determine what was being said or what was meant by what was being said.

"I know that I'm the younger grape here but I have just one thing to add. I know you're upset, but please don't eat us."

Just then, Emmy noticed a bright blue creature with feathers landing under the leaf.

"Emmy your spirit can soar high if you will only let Christ have His way with your heart."

With great delight, Emmy wondered what this creature was and how it was able to fly so high in the sky.

"Hey up there, what is your name?" inquired Emmy.

"Are you speaking to me?"

"Yes, who are you?"

"Some call me Jay and others, well they call me Blue Jay. They both work for me."
said Jay

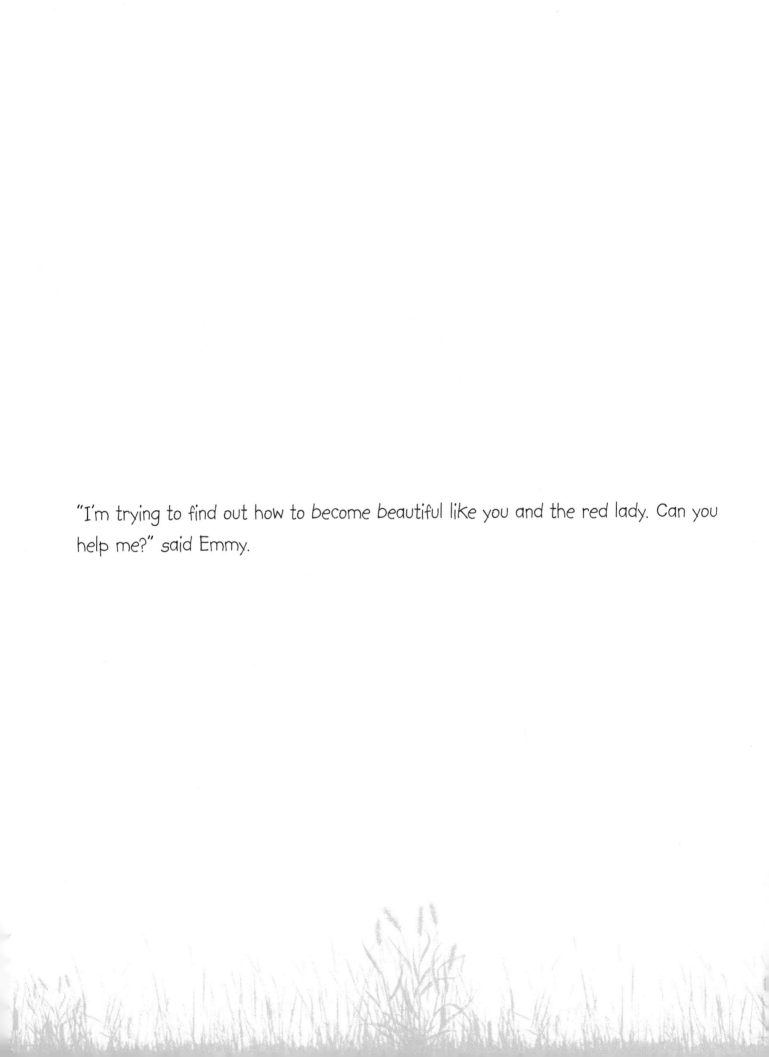

"I'm trying to find out how to become beautiful like you and the red lady. Can you help me?" said Emmy.

"No, I don't really know how myself, but, I have a friend who told me that I just need to be myself and that beauty will come from deep within."

"Who told you that?"

"Hummy"

"What is a Hummy?"

"Jay, he's quite flighty you know"

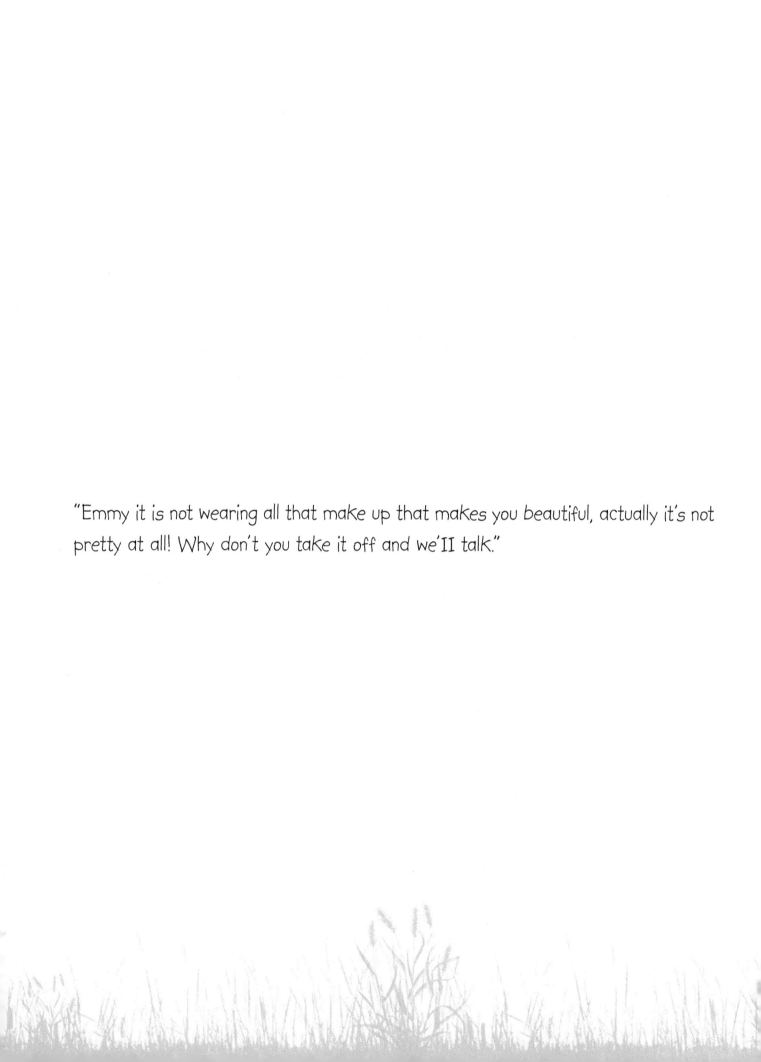

"Emmy it is not wearing all that make up that makes you beautiful, actually it's not pretty at all! Why don't you take it off and we'll talk."

"Then just be you! I find it's the only way to be."

"Thank you Hummy. Jay was right, you are a beautiful lady."

"It's just not possible even with all that make up on. You still look like a worm!"

"NOW WOULD YOU PLEASE MOVE ON? I have things to do."

She became very disheartened and wondered why it was that some had beauty and others could fly while she was stuck in the mud.

Emmy was beginning to feel rather sad inside. She felt like she would always be an ugly worm stuck in the dirt.

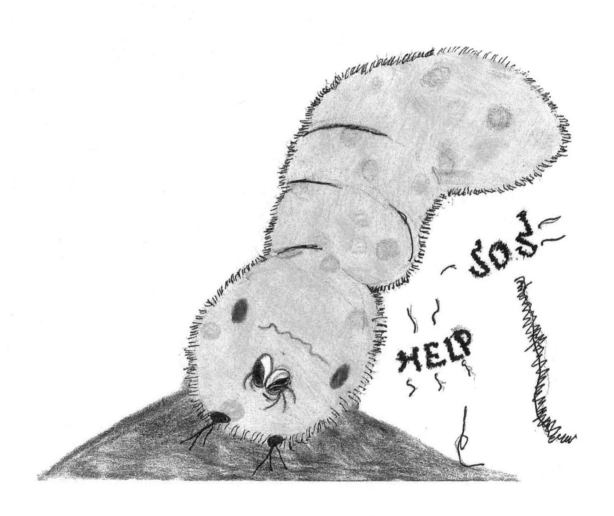

In a quest for comfort...

Her sadness seemed to make her hungry. She ate and ate for several months in a quest for something to make her feel better. Something that would set her free from the bondage she felt within.

She continued to feast her sorrows away. Months passed and Emmy seemed to become more and more discouraged. So great that it echoed into the untouchable places of her heart. She felt like she could not share this pain with anyone. She felt distraught inside and nothing could relieve the pain that seemed to consume her heart. She pondered life trapped inside her ugly hairy body.

Exhausted and alone, she curled up on a leaf and began to cry. Feeling it was too hard to continue, she considered her options. Emmy began thinking things through. While thinking, she overheard chatter coming from a nearby vine. She could not determine what was being said or what was meant by what was being said,

"I know I'm the younger one here but, I have just one thing to add. I know you're upset, but please don't eat us."

"Hey can I hang out with you two?"

"Sure we have bunches of fun. I'm a grape."

"I'm a grape too, what's wrong young lady?"

"Well…. I'm just so ugly, I don't want to be a hairy worm anymore, I want to be special, and I want to be beautiful."

"Look at me, you are beautiful! Now, put your thumb up and point it toward yourself. Now say I'm "thumb" buddy special."

"Ok. I'm "thumb" buddy special"

"Oh, yes you are! Now put that thumb up and say it."

"Ok, I'm "thumb" buddy special." Emmy muttered.

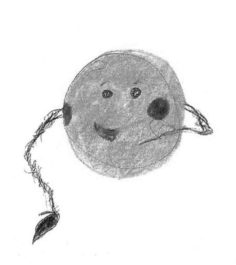

"Now you must believe it! And remember that God makes no mistakes and he certainly does not."

"Wow, thank you for caring about me, it's hard to believe to trust others and I've not been able to talk about these feeling of pain. You can't just cover it up."

"Emmy, what about all the people who love you, who need you?"

"Now put that thumb up and let me hear it again"

"I'M THUMBY SPECIAL!"

Emmy thanked her friend for caring and said goodnight.

Early the next morning, the spotted critter awoke to find the leaves not only covered with dew, but also something very colorful.

The intrigued little critter could not take her eyes off the lovely creature she saw through the early morning rays.

Just as she approached the elegant performer a large drop of dew fell from the leaf and landed on Emmy's head.

A dismal feeling of helplessness consumed Emmy to her core. It was at that very moment of despair that the skies opened up. Her new strength allowed her to look further and see a colorful performer above her that gave her the desire to press on.

Then she saw it, the most picturesque and exquisite sight Emmy had ever witnessed. There she was, sitting on a rose, sunning in the warmth of the morning light.

Emmy crawled closer to get a better look. She tried to sneak a peek from the lower leaf, but it was just too hard to see due to the early morning fog that darkened sky.

Driven by curiosity, the ugly caterpillar didn't notice or seem to mind her wet head. Intent on getting a closer look, she shook her head and dried her eyes.

As Emmy ventured closer, she experienced a heartfelt warmth radiating deep within her that she had never experienced before. The warmth beckoned her troubled heart to look further.

While Emmy was thinking on the beauty she so desired, she was quickly brought back to reality when another leaf shook and dropped more dew on the little wet caterpillar's head.

Shaking vigorously, the wet wild-haired worm worried that the beautiful creature might fly away.

Suddenly, from out of the sky, a voice came that seemed so peaceful that it warmed the heart of the frustrated caterpillar.

"Hey, what are you shaking about?"

"Who, me?"

"Yes, you, what is your name?"

"My name is Emmy Jo."

"Emmy it's not me, it's the Christ in me that makes one so beautiful. My name is Grace and I'm a butterfly. Believe it or not"

"I ONCE LOOKED JUST LIKE YOU!"

"What a beautiful name."

"Thank you, if only I were beautiful." Emmy sighed.

"Emmy you need to know that beauty comes from within and that it is God's grace that makes things beautiful, and only in God's time."

"Oh sweetheart you have to talk about it! You have to acknowledge the pain to heal. The real core of the pain has to come from the inside out to truly heal."

"Well, I've been on a journey to a place of peace. Please know that it is the journey, not the destination that brings the healing and peace into your life and prepares you for the ultimate destination known, which is heaven."

"You see, I once crawled on the ground in the dirt wondering how I could be transformed into something different."

"I hated myself and wanted to change; however, I did not want to go through the pain that is required for transforming into something beautiful that honors Christ."

"I did not want to feel any pain I just wanted it to go away. I learned very quickly that if I wanted to be transformed into something beautiful, I had to go through a metamorphosis."

"A whatphosis?" exclaimed Emmy.

"A metamorphosis is the changing from something ugly into something very beautiful."

"To help others to help you on the journey, it is ultimately in Him where you will find peace and comfort which will bring the beauty for which you desire."

"Are you ready for the journey?"

"Yes Grace, I am and thank you for being willing to be used of God to help others find the way that leads to a peace and beauty. But what if I can't go the distance? What If I don't make it?"

"You know Emmy, you are learning, but keep in mind that you will grow and mature. It is during their times that you will become stronger so that you can, in turn, help others to become beautiful in God's sight also."

While the journey seemed long and tiring, there were times of bliss when Emmy and Grace enjoyed happiness and times of laughter.

With great anticipation and excitement, the little frightened critter mustered up the strength to look beyond her dirty, hairy self and move forward.

"Hummy has a beauty that radiates from within. She will probably be humming by here soon; you'll hear her humming a ditty. Listen very closely she is fast."

So months passed and Emmy seemed to become more and more discouraged. Her disappointment turned into sorrow. Her pain seemed so great that it echoed into the untouchable placed of her very soul. She felt like she could not share this pain with anyone.

"Jesus will make all things beautiful in your life if you let Him in. He will cleanse you, save you and make all things beautiful in His time. He is why my spirit soars."

"Wow, thank you for caring about me. It's hard to trust others and I've not been able to talk about these feelings of pain."

"You can't just you know, we all have pain that we don't want to talk about and we only let a few others get close enough to help us. Christ died for us, now don't you think he also cares about you?"

"Emmy, what about all the people who love you?"

"Now put that thumb up and let me hear it again. I'm "thumb" buddy special."

Quietly and timidly Emmy pushed her way through the thick vine and leaves with great anticipation of getting closer to the colorful show ahead.

Grace helped her dear friend find the softest green leaf to craw upon and tucked her in with tenderness.

"Sweet dreams my dear friend sees you in the morning."

Feeling drained and empty, Emmy cuddled up on a fuzzy green leaf and fell fast asleep.

She just could not get the beautiful lady off her mind. "How can one become so beautiful?"

The next morning the spotted critter awoke to find not only with the dew,

But also with something very colorful.

The rays of the bright sun stretched out and reached down from heaven like God's loving arms wrapping rays around her filling her with the warmth and beauty of God's love.

They seemed to fill Emmy with warmth that gave her the strength to dig deeper and press on toward her quest for that beauty that she longed for.

Just as she approached the elegant performer. A large drop of morning dew fell from the leaf above her head and landed on Emmy's head.

The rays of the brilliant sun reminded Emmy of the heavenly father that her friends spoke of.

Emmy and Grace discovered that it was the inner beauty her friend possessed to which is just as promised Emmy. She found herself taking flight with all the grace and beauty she had ever imagined possible.

Full of admiration to her Lord, Emmy thanked God for freedom from the bondage she once knew.

She also thanked the Lord for the graces He honored her with throughout the seasons of her life.

It was that very day that Emmy determined in her heart to take flight and allow the Lord to use her life.

Emmy thanked God for her love and devotion of her new found friend.

Emmy dreamed of brilliant colors that night. Instead of the nightmares that used to engulf her sleep.

When Emmy awoke, she found herself breaking through the ugly gray cocoon of the past into a light, airy, beautiful butterfly.

She was breathless.

She found herself fluttering with joy, truly touched to awaken and find herself surrounded by all the "graces" that were so special to the beautiful fair winged lady.

Emmy thanked her new friends for caring and said goodnight.

CPSIA information can be obtained
at www.ICGtesting.com
Printed in the USA
BVHW022046010519
547089BV00024B/1035/P